For my two grandsons James and Nicholas Lincoln who live
far from the ocean but always near to my heart.
And to my niece Grace Jia, the beautiful adopted baby our family got to keep.
N.L.

For the dedicated biologists who make a difference
along the rocky coast of the Atlantic Ocean.
P.J.W.

www.bunkerhillpublishing.com

First published in 2005 by Bunker Hill Publishing Inc.
26 Adams Street, Charlestown, MA 02129 USA

10 9 8 7 6 5 4 3 2 1

Text © Nan Lincoln 2005
Illustration © Patricia J. Wynne 2005

All rights reserved

ISBN 1 59373 047 0

Designed by Louise Millar
Copyedited by George T. Kosar, PhD. The Sarov Press

Printed in China

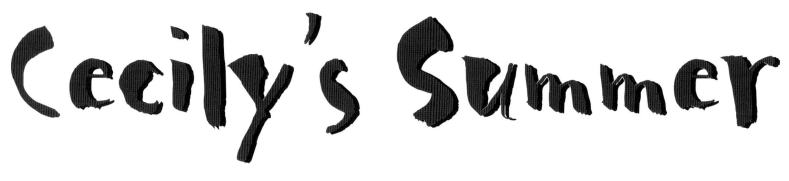

Cecily's Summer

written by **Nan Lincoln**

illustrated by **Patricia J. Wynne**

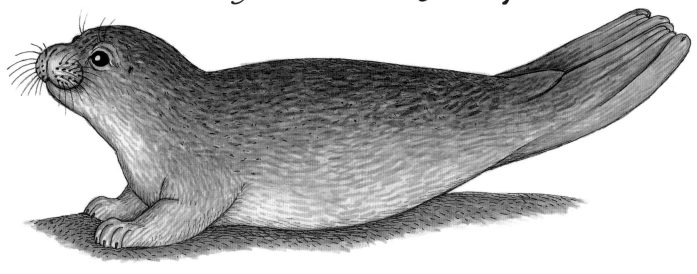

BUNKER HILL PUBLISHING

BOSTON

Cecily was born on a chilly spring day on a rocky reef off the coast of Maine. She did not have a name, then. She did not even know what she was. She was just one of many small furry creatures born on the reef that spring.

The first things Cecily saw were blue above and green below.

The blue was warm like the soft, furry sides of her mother. It was the sky.

The green was cold and wet like her mother's black nose when she nuzzled and sniffed her. It was the sea.

In between was hard and gray. It was the rocky reef where she was born.

Cecily liked the warm blue sky and her mother's warm, furry sides the best.

She was happy and thought she would stay under that blue sky forever, lying close to her mother's side, drinking her warm, fishy-tasting milk.

But one day something different happened.

Cecily was lying close to her mother's side when all of a sudden she heard a rumbling, roaring noise.

She looked out over the water and saw a scary thing. A sharp pointy thing was slicing through the green ocean with swirling, whirling blades. It was a boat.

The boat came closer and closer to the rocky reef, rumbling and roaring. *Urrrrr-Gurrrr-Rurrrr!*

There was a thumping and bumping on the reef and smack! something bumped into Cecily as it rushed by. She fell, rolling and tumbling down the rocky reef into the cold, green ocean.

Splash!

Whoop! Whoop! Cecily cried, Mother where are you?

But her mother did not come.

Cecily swam and swam through the cold, green ocean looking for her mother.

But she could not find her.

She saw a white thing floating in the water.

WHOOP! WHOOP! Cecily cried, have you seen my mother?

But the white thing just lifted its wings, cried *Keeya! Keeya!* and flew up into the blue sky. It was a seagull.

Cecily tried to follow the seagull into the sky, but her little flippers could not lift her out of the water.

She swam on and on.

After a while she saw three shiny black things swimming by, one after the other.

Whoop! Whoop! she called to them. Where is my mother?

But the black shiny things did not stop. They dove deep into the water and disappeared, then, appeared and disappeared again, their shiny, black backs humping and bumping through the green ocean. They were porpoises. Cecily tried to follow the porpoises but they did not wait for her. She swam on and on.

Something gray and blurry rolled over the blue sky and lay upon the surface of the water. It was fog.

Cecily looked this way and that way. She could not see the rocky reef where she was born. She could not see the seagull or the porpoises, she could not even see the blue sky. All she could see was gray. Cecily was lost in the gray and did not know which way to go.

Tired and hungry she stopped swimming and let the ocean carry her on and on.

After a long time floating on the ocean, Cecily felt something hard touch her flippers.

Is this my rocky reef? she wondered

It did not feel like her reef, but she flop-flopped out of the cold water onto a flat dry place. It was the shore.

Just ahead, through the blurry, gray fog, she saw a dark shape. *Whoop! Whoop!* she called out. "Is that you, Mother?"

The shape did not answer. When Cecily reached it she saw it was not her mother. It was just a big old rock covered with slimy seaweed.

Cecily was so tired and hungry she pretended the rock was her mother's warm sides. She huddled close and waited for her mother to find her.

While she waited she slept.

Ruff! Ruff! Ruff!

Cecily woke up and opened her eyes. She saw something big and furry staring at her, making loud noises and showing its pointy, white teeth. It was a dog.

Whoop! Whoop! Did my mother come yet? Cecily asked the dog. The dog did not answer. It ran away along the shore crying *Ruff! Ruff! Ruff!*

In a while something else came along the shore. It had long legs, and long arms and a roundish head with yellow fur on top, a pointy nose, a pink mouth and two blue eyes. It was a woman.

Whoop! Whoop! Cecily cried. I want my mother!

"I know you want your mother little one," the woman said. "I have been watching you for a long time. I have not seen your mother. But I will take good care of you. When you have grown big and strong you can go look for your mother again."

The woman bent her legs, reached out her arms, picked up the cold, wet little creature and wrapped her in a blanket.

Cecily felt warm as she lay in the woman's arms. She fell asleep and dreamed she was back on the rocky reef, huddled close to her mother's warm side drinking her warm fishy-tasting milk.

When Cecily woke up again, she did not know where she was. She looked about with her round black eyes and saw she was in a square place with high walls and a cover on top. It was a house. A house made of logs.

Cecily did not know about log houses but she did know that she was very, very hungry. *Whoop! Whoop!* she cried. I want food!

Pretty soon the woman appeared, she had something pink in her hand. It was a baby bottle. She sat down next to Cecily and put the bottle in her mouth.

Cecily did not understand. This was not how her mother fed her. The warm, creamy milk the woman squirted in her mouth did not taste like the milk her mother gave her.

Whoop! Whoop! she cried, turning her head away. I do not like this pink thing! I will not drink this yucky stuff!

Hours later, both Cecily and the woman were covered with creamy milk, but still Cecily would not drink from the bottle.

"I think you do not like the shape of this rubber nipple," the woman said. "I will try something different."

She left the room. When she came back she was holding a square, squishy thing. It was a sponge.

The woman cut a piece from the sponge and stuck it into the top of the bottle instead of the rubber nipple. This time when the bottle was put in Cecily's mouth she did not turn her head away.

The sponge nipple was not the same as her mother but she was very, very hungry and finally drank up two whole bottles of the creamy milk.

When her tummy was full she rolled over on her side to go to sleep.

"Good girl," the woman said. "You will be okay now and I will call you Cecily."

That is how Cecily got her name.

The next day when Cecily woke up and called out *Whoop! Whoop!* I'm hungry! the woman came with the pink bottle. But she was not alone. With her were three others and the dog with the pointy teeth. One of the others was tall, with fur on his face. It was a man. The other two were smaller, with smooth faces and yellow fur on the top of their heads. They were children, a little boy and a little girl. It was a family.

The little boy bent down close. "Hello Cecily," he said.

Tchoo! Tchoo! Cecily snorted, slapping her flippers on the floor, *Smack! Smack!* I do not know what you are, stay away!

She flop-flopped over to the woman and hid behind her legs.

"Cecily is scared and hungry," the woman told the family. "We will give her time to get to know us."

When the woman fed Cecily from the pink bottle with the sponge on top, it did not seem so strange and she drank the creamy milk right up. After Cecily finished her bottle she sniffed and snuffled the woman's arms and neck and face with her shiny black nose and stiff whiskers to learn what she smelled like and what she felt like.

The woman did not smell or feel like the mother Cecily remembered. And this was not the rocky reef where she was born. But she would stay with this woman, in this log house, with this family until she was big and strong enough to find her own family and her own home again.

Cecily grew bigger and stronger every day drinking the creamy milk from the bottle that the woman brought whenever she called out *Whoop! Whoop!*

At night when she called for her bottle, the woman would wrap them both up in a warm blanket and Cecily would drink her bottle while they watched flickering pictures coming from a little box. It was the Tonight Show on TV.

Cecily did not understand what the little man on the TV was saying, but she did like being cuddled in the warm blanket and the way the woman's tummy jiggled when she laughed at the little man.

In the daytime Cecily followed the woman out under the blue sky and played on tickling green stuff that surrounded the house. It was grass. She followed the woman into her garden and watched her plant peas, carrots, tomatoes, and corn. Sometimes she went for rides with the family in a big blue rumbly thing. It was a car.

Cecily waited in the car with the children when the woman went into the store to buy more cream for her bottles. *Whoop! Whoop!* she called when she thought the woman was taking too long. Sometimes the children called out *Whoop! Whoop!* too.

Cecily was happy. She thought she would stay here forever drinking her bottles, playing in the tickling, green grass, going for rides in the car, and watching TV.

She forgot about the cold, green ocean, the rocky reef where she was born. The loud, scary boat. She forgot about the warm, furry sides of her mother.

The days got warmer and warmer. It was summer. Sometimes when the woman was working in her garden Cecily slept in a little house the man built for her outside. It kept her out of the hot sun and away from the buzzing mosquitoes.

One day the woman said, "Cecily, you are big and strong enough now to learn how to swim in the ocean."

Cecily had grown too big to be carried, so the woman picked her up and put her into a rolling box on wheels. It was a wheelbarrow. *Whoop! Whoop!* Cecily called as they thumped and bumped down a path to the shore. This is fun!

When they reached the edge of the water the woman picked Cecily up out of the wheelbarrow and plopped her into the cold ocean water. Splash!

This was not fun at all! This was terrible! *Whoop! Whoop!* Cecily cried. Get me out of here!

Now Cecily remembered the ocean. She remembered how it had carried her away from her rocky reef and her mother. She wrapped her little flippers around the woman's legs and would not let go. She did not want to get lost again.

"We will try swimming another day," the woman said. She picked Cecily up and took her back up the path in the wheelbarrow.

But the same thing happened the next day. Every time Cecily was plopped into the cold, green ocean, she wrapped her flippers around the woman's legs and would not let go.

"Okay, Cecily," the woman said. "You are afraid of this cold ocean water, but you have to learn to swim, so we will try something different."

The next day the woman took Cecily to a different place. Not the ocean, but a place where the water was flat and blue. It was a lake.

She did not plop Cecily into the water. Instead the woman dove head first into the blue lake, and swam off just like a porpoise.

Whoop! Whoop! wait for me, Cecily cried and splashed into the water.

It was not so terrible. This water was warmer than the green ocean and the woman was right there with her, nose to nose.

Cecily remembered how to swim.

She flew through the blue water. She did a somersault, then a belly-roll. She dove deep, touched the woman's toes with her black nose, then flew to the surface and let her breath out *Brrrrsssh!* in a mist of sparkling spray.

Whoop! Whoop! she cried. Look at me, look at me!

Cecily played in the blue water until the woman got tired and rolled on her back to float.

Cecily was tired too. She climbed up on the woman's belly, put her head down and started to drift off to sleep.

This must be my mother now, Cecily thought as they floated together on the blue water of the lake.

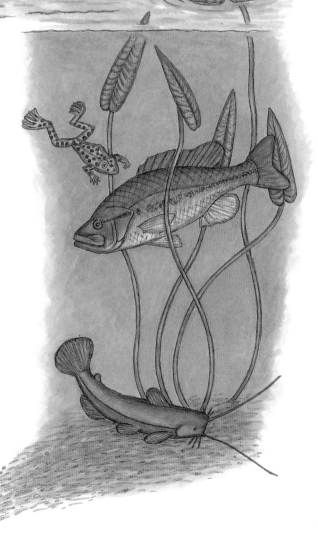

After that Cecily could not wait to go swimming in the lake. Let's go, let's go! she whooped every time she saw the woman change into her red bathing suit.

She loved to play games in the water with the whole family. She loved to dive between the man's legs, slip through the little boy's arms and bump the little girl along with her nose. When she was tired, Cecily climbed on the woman's belly or back and took a nap.

Cecily even liked swimming in the ocean now. She had grown fatter drinking all that creamy milk and the water did not feel so cold.

There was so much to see in the ocean.

There were purple starfish, squishy jelly fish, scuttling crabs, shiny pebbles, and snails of all different colors and shapes. Sometimes Cecily saw silvery little fish darting this way and that. She tried to catch up to them, but they were too fast.

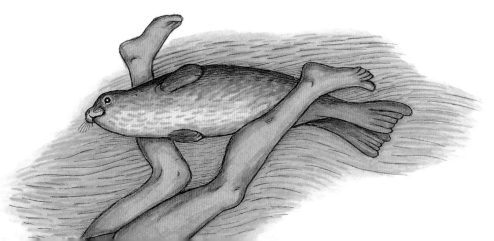

One warm summer day the woman had an idea. She went to a store and bought a snorkel and a face mask so she could swim in the ocean with Cecily underwater and see all the things she saw. But when Cecily saw the mask on the woman's face and the snorkel in her mouth she thought it was a scary monster.

She bumped them hard with her nose, and slapped them with her flippers.

Tchoo! Tchoo! she snorted. Get away from my mother!

The woman decided that a face mask and snorkel was not such a good idea after all.

Most of the time Cecily swam alone in the ocean. When she heard the woman call *"Cecileee!"* she knew it was time to come onto shore and there would be a bottle waiting for her.

Now the bottle was filled with yummy, lumpy milk that had fresh fish ground up in it. Cecily did not need the sponge anymore. She drank it right from the rubber nipple with a big hole cut through the top.

Cecily was happy. She thought she would stay like this forever. She would sleep in the log house with the woman and the family at night and in the day she would swim in the lake or the ocean under the warm blue sky. Some day, she thought, she would have long legs and long arms and yellow fur on her head, just like the woman.

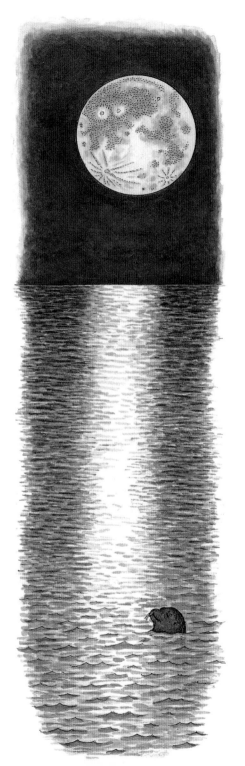

But then something different happened. After swimming in the ocean all day, the woman fed Cecily the bottle right there on the shore, but did not put Cecily in the wheelbarrow and bring her back to the log house for the night.

"Cecily," the woman said. "You are a good strong swimmer now. It is time for you to learn to sleep in the ocean. I will come back in the morning."

That night Cecily was not afraid. She felt safe in the water. She let the ocean rock her to sleep while floating in a path of light made by a big round circle of gold hanging above her in the black sky. It was the moon.

Cecily had drifted far out on the path of light. When she woke up the next morning she did not know where she was. She listened for the woman calling *"Cecileee!"* but did not hear her.

She did hear *Whoop! Whoop! Whoop!* coming from a big rocky reef sticking out of the green ocean. She swam over to find out what could be making such a strange noise.

Swimming in the water around the big rock were one, two, three, four, five little furry creatures with big, round eyes, shiny black noses, stiff whiskers, and flippers. They were harbor seal pups.

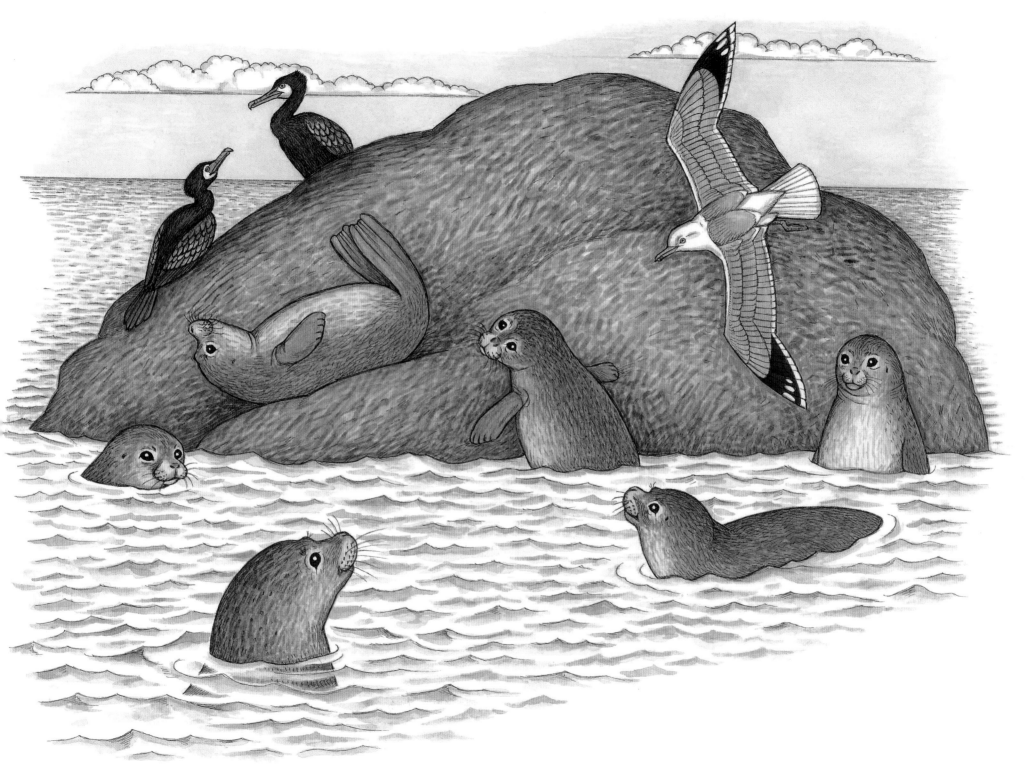

Cecily watched the seal pups rolling in the ocean, doing somersaults, diving down deep then flying to surface and letting their breath out *Brrrrsssh!*

Whoop! Whoop! one of them called when it saw Cecily. Come and play, come and play!

Cecily did not know what they were but it looked like they were having fun. So she joined them, rolling and diving in the green ocean.

She watched one of her new friends
chase after a darting fish, catch it, and swallow it whole.

All that playing made Cecily hungry, too. She tried chasing a
fish but could not catch it. She tried again and still the fish was
too fast for her. She tried one more time, pushing herself
through the water with her back flippers and steering with her
front flippers. This time she caught the darting fish and
swallowed it whole.

It was pretty good, but hard work and she was tired.

Where was the woman and her bottle of yummy, lumpy milk?

Cecily swam away from the rocky reef and the playful seal pups to go find the woman. The taste of the green ocean in her mouth and the tingles on her stiff whiskers told her which way to go.

In a while she heard *"Cecileee! Cecileee!"* and followed the sound of the woman's voice to the shore.

"This will be your last bottle, Cecily," the woman said. "The summer is almost over. You have grown big and strong and you are a very good swimmer now. You do not need me to feed you anymore. It is time for you to learn to live in the ocean."

After Cecily finished drinking her last bottle, the woman held her in her arms, and gently patted her dark, furry head.

"Thank you for letting me be your mother this summer, Cecily," she said. "I will always love you and remember you. But it is time to say good-bye."

The woman stood up and walked up the path toward the log house where her family was waiting.

Cecily did not understand.

Whoop! Whoop! she called, wait for me! and started to follow the woman up the path.

Then from out on the ocean she heard her new friends calling. *Whoop! Whoop! Whoop!* Come with us! Come with us!

Cecily looked one way, then she looked the other way. She did not know which way to go.

All of a sudden Cecily's big round eyes got bigger and rounder. Now she understood. It was then she realized she was meant to be in the ocean, not in a log house. She was meant to catch lots of fish, not drink from a pink baby bottle. She was meant to dive deep in the water to find scuttling crabs and purple starfish, not ride in a rumbly blue car. At night she was not meant to watch TV, but to sleep on rocky reefs under the gold moon.

Cecily knew what she was. She was a seal, not a human, and her family was calling her. It was time to go home. She flop-flopped back to the water's edge and dove into the beautiful green ocean, just like a seal pup is meant to do. *Whoop! Whoop!* she called to her family, Here I come!

The Real Story

The story of *Cecily's Summer* is true. In May of 1976, our dog Nahvoo found a baby harbor seal alone on the shore of Mount Desert Island, Maine, where I lived in a log house with my husband Bob and our two children, Benjamin and Alexandra. When it was certain the seal pup had been abandoned, I was given permission from the local wildlife warden to take care of her, with the understanding I would release her back to the wild when the time came.

Researchers at the local College of the Atlantic in Bar Harbor, which studies marine mammals, agreed to help. They gave me the recipe for Cecily's "creamy milk" and eventually told me when it was time to let her go.

The full story of that magical summer raising Cecily and returning her back to the wild seal colony is told in my book *The Summer of Cecily* (Bunker Hill, 2004).

Today abandoned seal pups are cared for and nurtured at marine rescue stations and aquariums before they are released into the wild. I like to think what I learned about feeding and caring for Cecily has helped these rescuers be successful in their efforts.

— NAN LINCOLN

Spotted seal

Hawaiian Monk seal

Bearded seal

Ringed seal

Did you know that?...

Weddel seal

Harp seal

- Harbor seal pups are always born in the spring.

- The rocky reef they are born on is called a rookery.

- The pups weigh fifteen to twenty pounds at birth.

- A mother seal's milk is mostly fat, so their pups put on weight fast to resist the cold water.

- Pups know how to swim from the moment they are born. But they like to ride on their mother's back or tummy when they get tired swimming.

- A mature harbor seal can weigh as much as 300 pounds.

Southern Elephant seal

Ribbon seal

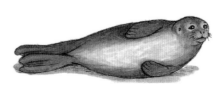

Baikal seal

Northern Elephant seal

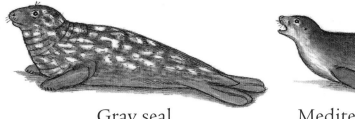

Gray seal

Mediterranean Monk seal

Caspian seal

Ross seal

- Harbor seals can stay underwater for as long as forty minutes and can dive as deep as 1,500 feet.

- Harbor seals can "taste" the water with their noses, mouths, and whiskers. This helps them find their way back to their rookery every spring.

Caribbean Monk seal

- Harbor seals are very curious and like to watch people on boats or on land from the safety of the water.

- Harbor seals can live as long as thirty-five years.

Hooded seal

- If anyone finds a baby seal alone on a beach they should leave it be and call their local wildlife warden or marine mammal rescue station.

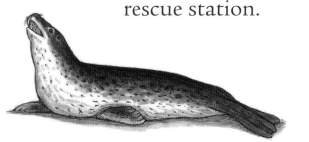

Leopard seal

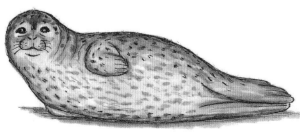

Harbor seal

Crabeater seal